DO YOU WANT A CAREER IN CRIMINAL JUSTICE?

JOBS IN THE JUVENILE JUSTICE SYSTEM

CORONA BREZINA

Published in 2022 by The Rosen Publishing Group, Inc.
29 East 21st Street, New York, NY 10010

Copyright © 2022 by The Rosen Publishing Group, Inc.

First Edition

Portions of this work were originally published as *Careers in the Juvenile Justice System*.

Library of Congress Cataloging-in-Publication Data

Names: Brezina, Corona, author.
Title: Jobs in the juvenile justice system / Corona Brezina.
Description: New York : Rosen Publishing, [2022] | Series: Do you want a career in criminal justice? | Includes bibliographical references and index.
Identifiers: LCCN 2021005329 | ISBN 9781499470147 (library binding) | ISBN 9781499470130 (paperback) | ISBN 9781499470154 (ebook)
Subjects: LCSH: Juvenile justice, Administration of--Vocational guidance--United States--Juvenile literature. | Law enforcement--Vocational guidance--United States--Juvenile literature. | Criminal justice personnel--United States--Juvenile literature.
Classification: LCC HV9104 .B744 2022 | DDC 331.7/61364360973--dc23
LC record available at https://lccn.loc.gov/2021005329

Some of the images in this book illustrate individuals who are models. The depictions do not imply actual situations or events.

Manufactured in the United States of America

CPSIA Compliance Information: Batch #CSRYA22. For further information contact Rosen Publishing, New York, New York at 1-800-237-9932.

Find us on

CONTENTS

INTRODUCTION

Criminal justice is an exciting field with a broad range of potential career paths for job seekers interested in pursuing work that's both highly challenging and immensely rewarding. The criminal justice system is made up of agencies and departments charged with preventing and punishing crime. Within the criminal justice system, the juvenile justice system deals out justice to young offenders.

The first juvenile court in the United States was established in 1899. Reformers believed juveniles should be rehabilitated, not tried and punished as adults. The separation between the two courts is based on the idea that young offenders are fundamentally different from adults. They lack adult maturity. They're more susceptible to peer pressure. Their characters are still being formed, and neuroscience has shown that the teenage brain is still building new connections. Thus, they're not fully responsible for their behavior.

Today, most young offenders still are dealt with by a juvenile court that's separate from adult criminal court. The juvenile justice system offers the opportunity for intervention rather than punishment. Most delinquent behavior has a root cause, such as family situations, mental illness, conflicts at school, substance abuse, or gang involvement. The juvenile justice system is designed to provide the means of changing an offender's attitude and behavior by addressing these underlying factors.

Juvenile justice is an ideal career choice for people who want to see justice served but also want to make a difference in children's lives. There are many different career paths in juvenile justice. Law enforcement officers, lawyers, judges, court staff, correctional officers, probation officers, counselors, educators, child welfare workers, and policy makers all have a stake in the juvenile justice system. Juvenile justice is a field that carries great responsibilities—it determines the future of many youth—but it also provides great rewards.

Youth under 18 who commit criminal offenses are dealt with by the juvenile justice system. Each state has a juvenile code made up of the laws relevant to minors.

CHAPTER 1

THE JUVENILE JUSTICE SYSTEM

The juvenile justice system deals with young people who are detained for delinquent behavior. This means that if they had been adults and arrested for the same offense, they would be considered criminals. Adults are dealt with in the criminal justice system. Young people are dealt with in the juvenile justice system. In addition to delinquents, the juvenile justice system has jurisdiction over neglected and dependent children, children involved in custody settlements, special needs children, and any other juvenile involved in legal proceedings. (Dependent children are children whose parents are unable to care for them.)

Law enforcement officers may take a juvenile offender into custody. They also have the option of issuing a citation or warning and releasing him or her.

Every day, over 2,000 young people are processed in the juvenile justice system. An offender may be taken into custody and assessed at intake, in which juvenile court officers decide how to proceed with the case. The offender may go to court and have a disposition handed down. The most common disposition is some form of probation.

The juvenile justice system uses terminology intended to avoid negative connotations associated with the criminal justice system. When the first juvenile court systems were established, reformers wanted to emphasize rehabilitation of young people rather than punishment. Therefore, juveniles are "taken into custody" rather than arrested. If they're "adjudicated delinquent," which is equivalent to being found guilty, they receive a "disposition" rather than a sentence.

JUVENILE JUSTICE SYSTEM CASE FLOW

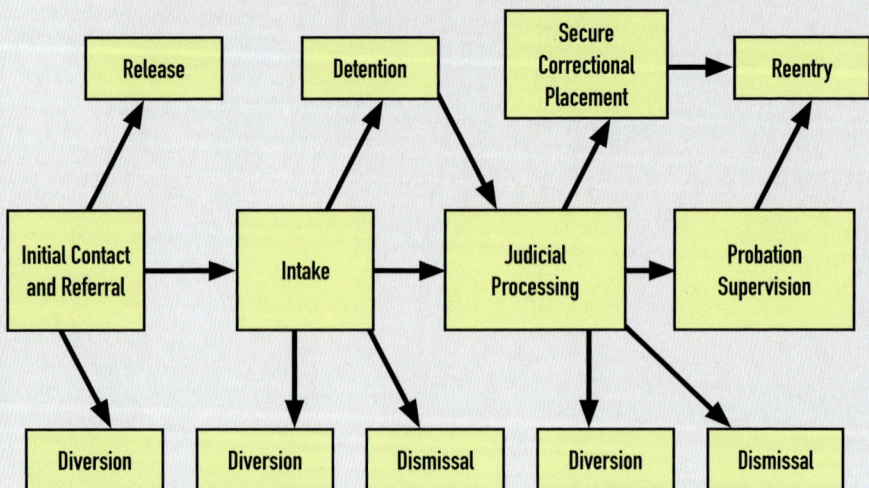

HANDING DOWN JUSTICE

According to the Office of Juvenile Justice and Delinquency Prevention, about 700,000 juveniles were arrested in 2019. This was the lowest number since the office began tracking data in 1980. The number of cases rose steadily in the 1980s and 90s, peaking in 1996, when about 2.7 million youth were arrested. The figure has declined ever since. Numbers fell by 67 percent between 2006 and 2019. According to the National Center for Juvenile Justice, in 2018 (the most recent year with available data), about 30 percent of juvenile delinquency cases ended with an adjudication of delinquency or transfer to criminal court, with a total of 220,000 cases adjudicated delinquent.

From 2009 to 2018, the highest number of juvenile delinquency cases (232,400) fell into the category of violent offenses, such as criminal homicide (1,100 cases), rape, robbery, and assault. The largest number were for simple assault (146,800), a lesser offense than aggravated assault (26,100). The next highest category, at 225,900 cases, was property offenses, such as burglary, larceny-theft, arson, vandalism, or trespassing. Then, there were 185,100 public order offenses, which include criminal behavior such as obstruction of justice, disorderly conduct, weapons offenses, and liquor law violations. There were also 101,000 drug law violations. Fifty-three percent of juvenile justice cases in 2018 involved youth under the age of 16.

Statistics concerning older teens are inconsistent because, in some states, adolescents over the age of 16 are tried in adult criminal court.

In 2018, 57 percent of juvenile justice cases were handled formally—the juvenile went before a judge in court. The remaining cases were handled informally, a practice usually called diversion. Serious offenses were more likely to be handled formally than lesser offenses in every category. Among property offenses, for example, 76 percent of motor vehicle theft cases, but only 50 percent of larceny-theft cases, were handled formally. Among person crimes, 72 percent of aggravated assault cases, but only 50 percent of simple assault cases, were handled formally. Drug offenses were an exception compared to all other categories of crime that are more likely to be handled formally than informally—only 47 percent were handled formally. The proportion of cases handled formally has been increasing since 2005, with the exception of drug offenses.

Trends in juvenile justice tend to shift depending on patterns of delinquency. During the mid-1990s, delinquency rates increased and led to public outcry that the juvenile system was too lenient on offenders. As a result, policies shifted toward stiffer penalties emphasizing punishment rather than rehabilitation. Delinquency rates have subsequently fallen, however, and there has been a shift in policies toward a recognition that juveniles are fundamentally different from adults. Research in neuroscience and developmental psychology have shown that the adolescent brain is still developing, and that youth lack impulse control, mature judgment, and understanding of the consequences of their actions. In some major court cases, these factors have led to a reduction of penalties for young offenders.

The total number of cases adjudicated delinquent has fallen steadily over the past 15 years, from 540,900 in 2005, to 220,000 in 2018. The decline was seen in all categories of offenses. The proportion of cases adjudicated delinquent fell, as well—in 2005, 61 percent of cases were adjudicated delinquent, compared with 52 percent in 2018.

Myths and Facts About Juvenile Justice

Myth: Some youths are remorseless "superpredators" with violent tendencies.

Fact: During the mid-1990s, some criminologists predicted a wave of young criminals would lead to skyrocketing crime rates. As a result, most states adopted harsher treatment of young offenders, with many increasing the number of youth transferred to adult court. Juvenile crime rates began a steady decline, however, disproving the "superpredator" theory. Some criminologists admitted they had been mistaken.

Myth: If a teen commits a crime, he or she should receive the same penalty as an adult who commits the same crime.

Fact: The juvenile justice system emphasizes rehabilitation rather than punishment, unlike the adult criminal justice system. Studies in neuroscience have shown that youths lack adult maturity and capacity for judgment, along with other differences in the brain. Landmark court cases have observed that youth have a greater chance of reforming than adults.

Myth: Kids in the juvenile system aren't entitled to a lawyer, or else they don't need one.
Fact: Youths who've been arrested have a right to legal counsel. In many cases, an experienced juvenile defense attorney can advocate for the teen's rights and help families navigate the judicial justice system.

SPECIAL CONSIDERATIONS FOR JUVENILES

The exact age range of a juvenile varies from one state to another. In most states, offenders under the age of 18 are sent to juvenile, rather than adult, court. In other states, anyone under the age of 16 is considered a juvenile. Some states also have an "age of responsibility," which ranges from 6 to 10. Anyone under this age is considered unable to understand the consequences of his or her actions.

Likewise, different states apply different definitions of delinquency. In addition to criminal acts, some states consider acts such as truancy (skipping school), curfew violation, and liquor possession to be delinquency. The offenses in this category, called status offenses, are illegal only because of the offender's underage status.

In some jurisdictions, children and teens who stay out past a certain hour can be detained for a curfew violation, which is a status offense.

Most young offenders enter the juvenile justice system when police or other law enforcement officials bring them in. Many large police departments have specialized juvenile crime units to deal with young offenders. A case may come to the attention of the police when the offenders are caught in the act or are reported by a victim or witness. In other cases, they may choose to turn themselves in. For very minor offenses, especially when the juvenile has no prior record, the officer may just issue a warning. For more serious offenses, the officer may issue a citation or take the offender to a juvenile detention facility.

If there have been formal measures taken against the offender, the case will go to a court intake officer. The intake officer may choose to dismiss or divert the case. Diversion of the case means the offender is dealt with informally without going before a court. For example, the offender might agree to a period of probation or community service.

Alternately, the intake officer may request a formal adjudication hearing—the juvenile justice

Jake Evans attends a hearing in 2015 in adult court in Weatherford, Texas. He pleaded guilty to the 2012 killing of his mother and younger sister.

system equivalent of a criminal trial—or recommend that the case be transferred to adult court. In some cases, the offender is held in short-term detention until the hearing. This may be for the good of the community, for the juvenile's own well-being, to allow for further testing and evaluation, or to make sure that the offender will attend the hearing. More often, the juvenile is released to a parent or guardian.

At the adjudication hearing, the offender goes before a judge. The proceedings are entered on the offender's court record. Many cases are uncontested, which means the offender doesn't deny the charges. If this is the case, the offender may make a plea bargain in return for a more lenient punishment.

If the allegations are found to be true, the judge hands out the disposition in a separate disposition hearing, which is the equivalent to sentencing in adult court. Most often, the delinquent receives probation. The disposition may include fines, restitution (paying back victims), or community service. The offender may be referred to counseling for mental health or behavioral issues. For serious mental health disorders, he or she may be sent to a mental hospital. Some offenders may be conditionally freed but restricted by house arrest, electronic monitoring, attendance at a day treatment program, or other probation requirements. An offender may be placed in a foster home or other residential facility. The most serious offenders may be sent to facilities such as state schools, boot camps, or other institutions.

Delinquents who've been through the juvenile justice system—in particular, those who've spent time in a juvenile institution—are released for aftercare, which is the equivalent of parole. If they're picked up for another offense after they've been formally discharged, the system will probably deal with them more harshly the next time around.

INDIVIDUALIZED JUSTICE

Many of the children and teens handled in the juvenile justice system are highly vulnerable. They come from disadvantaged backgrounds, and many are people of color. They're more likely to have learning disabilities, suffer from mental illness, or deal with substance abuse issues than the average youth. Many have experienced hardships during their lives such as abuse, neglect, violence, and family trauma.

A "one-size-fits-all" approach such as confinement in a large correctional institution is unlikely to consider each youth's particular needs and circumstances. Since the early 21st century, juvenile justice court professionals have emphasized the importance of matching youth to appropriate services. In its Enhanced Juvenile Justice Guidelines, the National Council of Juvenile and Family Court Judges (NCJFCJ) notes that, "Although fewer violent and dangerous crimes are being committed by youth, more youth are being referred to juvenile justice courts for drugs, domestic violence, and other problem behaviors that can be handled more effectively through social, substance abuse, and mental health agencies." The group recommends that such cases be dealt with through informal intervention rather than formal proceedings before the juvenile justice court.

REHABILITATION AND REINTEGRATION

To some extent, the juvenile justice system runs parallel to the adult criminal justice system, but there are key differences. Many of these differences stem from the basic goals of the two systems. In general, the juvenile justice system aims to rehabilitate offenders, while the adult criminal justice system exists to punish offenders.

The difference between the systems begins with language. From intake to aftercare, the juvenile justice system involves specialized terminology that distinguishes it from the adult criminal justice system. Juveniles aren't "arrested"; they're "taken into custody." Prosecutors don't charge them with a "crime"; they file a "petition" with the juvenile court. Offenders aren't convicted and "found guilty"; they're "adjudicated delinquent." They don't go to "jail" or "prison"; they're "placed in an institution," such as a reform school or other state-operated juvenile facility.

Generally, a judge decides juvenile cases. Adult criminals have the constitutional right to trial by jury. Juvenile adjudication hearings are sometimes less formal than adult trials. The juvenile justice system was founded on the parens patriae principle. This is a "country as parent" philosophy, meaning it's the duty of the government to act in the best interests of children who come before the court. Although approaches to juvenile justice have in some ways evolved away from these roots, the juvenile court judge is still expected to approach the case from the viewpoint of a wise and concerned parent. Unless the charge is serious, the hearing may take the form of an inquiry, rather than a tense legal battle. Nonetheless, it follows the same basic procedures as a criminal trial: presentation of evidence, testimony of witnesses, closing arguments by the prosecutor and defense lawyer, and so on. Unlike criminal trials, which are open to the public, proceedings in juvenile court are usually confidential.

The judge can take the offender's social history into account in choosing the disposition. This differs from adult criminal trials, in which the verdict rests only on the legal facts of the case. Before making a decision, the judge may consult a pre-disposition report on the juvenile offender prepared by a probation officer. Significant factors could include family life, history of abuse, psychiatric conditions, and prior juvenile record. Based on the facts of the case and these special considerations, the judge decides on an appropriate disposition. The judge has considerable leeway in imposing a disposition. The judge chooses a disposition that he or she believes would be most likely to rehabilitate the offender while maintaining public safety.

Juveniles can be tried for status offenses, which are not considered criminal behavior in adult court. In addition, the offender's parents can sometimes be held responsible for his or her behavior. For example, parents may be penalized for their child's truancy. Some states fine or jail adults who provide

An offender attends a felony assessment with judicial specialist Maryann Peratt at the Jefferson County Juvenile Assessment Center in Golden, Colorado.

alcohol to minors subsequently involved in drunk driving accidents.

Despite the differences between the two justice systems, juveniles have many of the same rights as adults. Police must inform juveniles of their constitu-

LANDMARK CASE: *ROPER V. SIMMONS*

Christopher Simmons was tried as an adult in a Missouri court for a murder he committed when he was 17 years old. He was found guilty and sentenced to death for the crime.

At the time, the United States was one of the few countries in the world that executed offenders for crimes committed when they were juveniles. In the 1989 case of *Stanford v. Kentucky*, the U.S. Supreme Court found that it wasn't unconstitutional to execute offenders who were as young as 16 years old when they committed the crime.

In 2003, Simmons' lawyers appealed the sentence, arguing that the *Stanford v. Kentucky* ruling should be overturned. They challenged the death penalty for offenders who committed crimes as juveniles on the grounds that it constituted cruel and unusual punishment.

In the landmark *Roper v. Simmons* ruling in 2005, the U.S. Supreme Court reversed *Stanford v. Kentucky*, ending the death penalty for offenders under the age of 18. The court found that due to "evolving standards of decency," executing young offenders did constitute cruel and unusual punishment, prohibited by the Eighth Amendment of the Constitution. The judges also pointed out that juveniles are psychologically different from adults. They lack maturity, are more vulnerable to influences such as peer pressure, and haven't yet developed a fully formed character. The court also noted that most other countries overwhelmingly prohibited the death penalty for juveniles.

tional rights before an interrogation. This is known as the Miranda warning. Juveniles have certain rights during their trial—sometimes with limitations—such as the right to a lawyer and the right to protection against self-incrimination (granted by the Fifth Amendment of the U.S. Constitution) and double jeopardy (being tried twice for the same charge). Like adults accused of a crime, young offenders also must be proven guilty beyond a reasonable doubt in court.

Many key issues in the juvenile justice system have been decided through rulings by the U.S. Supreme Court in Washington, D.C.

WORKING IN JUVENILE JUSTICE

Pursuing a career in the juvenile justice system can be both challenging and rewarding. A capable caseworker, an inspiring teacher, a passionate attorney, or any of the other professionals involved in juvenile justice can change a young person's life. Their work can open up a new future for juveniles involved in the system.

For a job seeker considering a career in juvenile justice, there's a huge range of opportunities. Prosecutors, caseworkers, probation officers, correctional officers, and many of the other people involved in the administration of juvenile justice are directly employed by the court or by state or local agencies. There are also many community organizations and other groups that reach out to young people through prevention, intervention, and outreach efforts. In addition, juvenile justice policies and programs are constantly being reevaluated and refined. Passionate individuals interested in revitalizing the system might choose to get involved in some of the innovative approaches that integrate new ideas about implementing juvenile justice.

A juvenile justice career isn't for everyone. Anyone interested in the field must be enthusiastic about working with young people. He or she must be able to forge a connection with teens and children who may come from a difficult background, have substance abuse or psychological issues, or present other challenges. Juvenile justice workers must be able to work well with others. A single case can involve interaction with representatives from many different agencies and organizations, as well as with people from the youth's family, school, and community. Sometimes, the work can be frustrating or overwhelming.

However, a juvenile justice career is highly rewarding. Many people who work in juvenile justice are passionate about helping young people and achieve the satisfaction of knowing they can make a difference through their work. The job outlook is also bright for most careers within the field, from counseling to law enforcement to legal professions.

CHAPTER 2

JOBS IN JUVENILE COURT

L egal professionals such as lawyers, judges, and juvenile court personnel are responsible for the process that determines whether a youth is delinquent and for deciding a disposition. If a youth's case is handled formally, the offender is scheduled for an adjudication hearing before a judge in juvenile court. Every state has at least one juvenile court, sometimes called a family court, circuit court, or probate court. In large cities, the courtroom is part of a dedicated juvenile justice center. In less densely populated areas, juvenile hearings are held in the county courthouse.

Jurisdiction over juvenile justice cases varies from one state to the next. Many states have different juvenile courts for different categories of cases. One court might hear cases involving serious delinquency offenses, for example, while a different court hears cases involving status offenses. And still another hears custody disputes involving parents or guardians.

As might be expected, most of the people who work for the juvenile court have a background in law. The National Council of Juvenile and Family Court Judges also recommends in its Enhanced Juvenile Delinquency Guidelines that court staff also be trained to "understand adolescent development and hold youth accountable in developmentally appropriate ways." In addition, the court system requires administrators and other personnel to handle the management of the court.

EARNING YOUR LAW DEGREE

The path to becoming a lawyer requires hard work, academic excellence, and dedication. Ideally, it should also include a fairly clean record—candidates for the bar generally undergo a background check that will uncover any past criminal activities, arrest records, credit problems, or ethical violations.

A young adult who wants to be an attorney can begin preparing in high school by receiving a well-rounded education and maintaining good grades. Lawyers need strong public-speaking, writing, research, problem-solving, and analytical skills. Students can take classes or participate in extracurricular activities that will help them to develop these

Anybody considering law school should be enthusiastic about spending long hours studying. Competition for admission is intense—good grades and a high LSAT score will improve chances of acceptance.

skills. High school students also may consider taking on summer jobs or doing volunteer work related to the legal system or public service.

A student must earn a bachelor's degree before attending law school. Although some colleges and universities offer pre-law programs, law schools don't require any specific major. A student may choose a liberal arts major broadly applicable to law, such as philosophy or history. He or she also may choose a major applicable to a specialized field of law, such as economics or computer science. Even if the undergraduate major has no direct connection to law, what matters most is maintaining a good academic record. Law schools also require that applicants take the Law School Admission Test (LSAT).

Once in law school, students choose a specific field of study. Those interested in juvenile justice should choose an area that's in some way relevant to the juvenile justice system. Areas of specialized study include family law, public interest law, and criminal law. In some law schools, students can enroll in a juvenile justice or family court clinic, where, under the supervision of clinic faculty and staff, they provide legal assistance to juveniles.

Law students generally complete their Juris Doctor (J.D.) degrees in three years. Before starting to practice law, however, the graduate must take the state bar exam and a national ethics exam. Upon passing both of these, he or she receives a license from the state to practice law.

According to the Occupational Outlook Handbook, the median annual wage for lawyers was $122,960 in 2019. Employment in the field was projected to increase 4 percent from 2019 to 2029, which is an average rate for all occupations.

PROSECUTING ATTORNEYS

Attorneys typically function as both advisers and advocates in legal matters. Advocates are people who argue on their clients' behalf and represent their best interests. They serve their client's interests by providing legal guidance and suggesting what steps to take in legal matters. They also act as their client's advocate in court, representing their case before a judge. For prosecuting attorneys, their client is the government—on a federal, state, or local level—and they're employed to present the case against offenders. Since juveniles are very rarely prosecuted in federal court, most are tried under state juvenile justice systems.

In adult criminal court, there's often an adversarial relationship between prosecuting and defense attorneys. Prosecutors want the defendant brought to justice, while defenders represent their client's interests. There's a different dynamic in juvenile court. Ideally, everybody involved in a juvenile justice case works to bring about a disposition that is most beneficial for the juvenile.

One of the prosecutor's most important duties is that of gatekeeper, in a sense, to the courtroom. The prosecutor is one of the key figures in deciding whether a case should be given an adjudication hearing. Alternatives include diversion or transfer of the juvenile to adult criminal court. A prosecutor can file a waiver with the juvenile court judge requesting that the juvenile be transferred to adult court. In some states, the prosecutor can directly file the case to adult criminal court.

For cases that are formally handled in court, the prosecutor prepares a case against the juvenile and presents it before the judge. He or she introduces

Although juvenile court procedures are similar to those of adult criminal trials, prosecutors and defense attorneys are less adversarial and more cooperative in a juvenile courtroom.

evidence, which can include physical evidence and witness testimony. The prosecutor examines the witnesses—asks questions—and then the defense attorney cross-examines the witnesses. The adjudication ends with the prosecution presenting closing arguments, followed by the defense attorney's closing arguments, and then a final rebuttal (response) by the prosecution. In some states, the prosecution also participates in the disposition hearing.

IS THE TEEN JURY IN?

Just like adults, juveniles have the right to a trial by jury. In some states, however, some offenders have the diversion option of teen court, sometimes called youth court or peer jury. Usually, only first-time offenders charged with minor offenses are eligible. They're given the option of teen court as an alternative to a formal court process. Generally, the judge, prosecutors, defenders, and jury are all made up of youth volunteers, although some models include an adult judge. The offender is often required to admit guilt before having the hearing. Typical sanctions include community service, writing letters of apology, or counseling. Teen courts generally are run by local law enforcement departments or juvenile courts. Sometimes, they operate in schools.

Teen courts turn peer pressure into a positive influence. The participants learn about civic responsibility, the legal process, and how the law is interpreted and applied. The program raises awareness of juvenile justice issues in the community. Often, offenders who go before teen court are encouraged or required to continue to participate as volunteers. Research has shown that recidivism rates are lower for offenders who are dealt with in teen court— they're less likely to commit future offenses. This may be because the teens selected for teen court are usually less likely to break the law again.

A first-time offender accused of shoplifting faces the judge in a La Plata, Maryland, teen court, in which first-time minor offenders appear before a jury of peers.

DEFENSE ATTORNEYS

In 1967, the Supreme Court case of *In re Gault* transformed how the juvenile justice system handled young offenders accused of juvenile delinquency. Three years earlier, 15-year-old Gerald Gault had been taken into custody for making obscene phone calls to a neighbor. His parents were not informed of his detention and upcoming adjudication, and the neighbor never appeared to testify in court. Gault was found delinquent and committed to the state reform school until the age of 21. He appealed the case. Eventually, the Supreme Court overturned the conviction, ruling that juveniles facing institutional confinement—the juvenile justice system's equivalent of jail time—are entitled to certain constitutional rights, including the right to an attorney. Juvenile proceedings after *In re Gault* came to resemble adult criminal trials more closely.

Juvenile justice defense lawyers represent their clients from the early stages of the case, such as initial police interrogation, through the adjudication and disposition hearing, as well as in any appeals or proceedings regarding probation violations. They may advise their clients on whether to settle for diversion or a plea bargain rather than exercise the right to have the case handled formally with an adjudication. At the adjudication, the defense attorney presents evidence that supports the client's case after the prosecution has rested. At the disposition hearing, the defense attorney may argue for a lighter punishment. The attorney may also attend subsequent court proceedings, such as reviews of plea agreement compliance or expungement hearings. At hearings on expungement of their juvenile record, delinquents who've met their obligations or have "aged out" of the juvenile justice system can ask to have their records sealed or erased.

Lawyers representing juveniles should be experienced in working with young offenders and be familiar with the procedures of the juvenile justice system (which do not always match up with those of the adult criminal justice system). Defense attorneys tend to take one of two approaches toward representing juvenile clients. They may take on a quasi–social worker role, in which they work with the prosecutor, probation officer, and other parties toward a solution that's in the client's best interest, even if the juvenile might consider it a punishment. On the other hand, they might vigorously defend the case and push for acquittal, much as they would represent an adult in criminal court.

An offender and her attorney prepare for court. Many delinquents who cannot afford to hire a lawyer are represented by court-appointed public defenders.

Some families hire a private defense attorney for an accused juvenile offender. If they can't afford to do so, then the court will appoint a juvenile public defender to represent them. Some juvenile defender programs provide highly trained and motivated defense lawyers for offenders. But many juvenile public defenders carry huge caseloads and don't have access to adequate resources. In addition, they often lack specialized training in juvenile justice.

JUVENILE COURT JUDGES

Juvenile court and family court judges are either elected or appointed to their positions. A judge must have a law degree, and most judges establish a distinguished background practicing in the field of law before becoming a judge.

In the juvenile justice system, judges are responsible for far more than presiding over the bench. They may be in charge of overseeing the budget, hiring personnel, and setting rules. They might personally supervise case scheduling and other tasks. In some courts, they may delegate these administrative responsibilities to other court personnel.

The judge has the final authority over a juvenile's fate. If a prosecutor has requested a waiver to adult court, the judge makes a decision on whether to grant it. In the courtroom, the judge maintains order and makes rulings on various issues—for example, if evidence is admissible—during the adjudication hearing. At the end of the adjudication, he or she

A family court judge signs a court order. Family court deals with cases such as divorce, child custody, and domestic violence.

determines whether the juvenile has engaged in delinquent conduct. Before the disposition hearing, the judge meets with the probation officer assigned to the case to review additional information, such as the juvenile's social history, which is sometimes compiled in a pre-disposition report. At the disposition hearing, the judge hands down the final punishment.

Ideally, on top of legal knowledge, a juvenile court judge should be familiar with child and adolescent development, community and social welfare services in the area, and the appropriate rehabilitation measures for different scenarios. Some experts have advised that juvenile judges serve for two years, three years, six years, or even longer. In reality, though, many juvenile courts don't mandate any particular experience or training for judges. In some jurisdictions, judges are assigned to juvenile courts for just six months or a year.

According to the Occupational Outlook Handbook, the median annual wage for law judges, adjudicators, and hearing officers was $97,870 in 2019, and the median annual wage for judges, magistrate judges, and magistrates was $136,910. Employment was projected to increase 2 percent from 2019 to 2029, which was slightly below the average rate for all occupations.

JUDICIAL DISCRETION

Juvenile court judges possess a great deal of judicial discretion—the power to issue a ruling based on what he or she deems fair considering the circumstances of the case. Judicial discretion allows the judge to issue a disposition intended to help each individual offender to achieve a positive outcome toward rehabilitation.

Judges base their decisions on relevant laws as well as the unique facts of the case. They document the specific factors that influenced their ruling. But broad judicial discretion can allow for unconscious bias to influence their decisions. For example, they may tend to hand down harsher dispositions for boys than girls in similar cases. Judicial discretion can also contribute to a lack of consistency in rulings across the juvenile justice system.

IN THE BEST INTEREST OF THE CHILD

A juvenile court judge from Ohio, Denise Navarre Cubbon, oversees a meeting to check in with a juvenile offender in her courtroom in Lucas County.

OTHER JOBS IN THE JUVENILE JUSTICE SYSTEM

In addition to the lawyers and the judge, there are a number of personnel who handle the many aspects of the administration and organization of the juvenile court. Some of the individuals who work with young people and their families are directly employed by the juvenile court. Others, such as specialists in various diversion programs or mental health professionals, work for social service agencies or other organizations.

The organization of the juvenile justice system varies from state to state. One state's juvenile court may have an assortment of directors, coordinators, executives, superintendents, managers, supervisors, and specialized officers that don't have exact equivalents in other states' courts. Instead of focusing on job titles, a job seeker in the field should look closely at the responsibilities and requirements for each position.

Most of these positions require a background in law, criminal justice, social work, or other relevant fields. For jobs that require working with juveniles, the employer generally requires a background check. In some areas, being bilingual often gives the applicant an edge.

After a young person is referred to the juvenile justice system, he or she is screened in a process called intake, which is handled by the intake officer. Intake is not the same as "booking" a criminal. Instead, intake usually takes the form of a prescheduled conference with the juvenile and his or her parents. The intake officer decides whether the offender should be dismissed, diverted, or scheduled for an adjudication hearing. In most cases, the intake officer is a probation officer or prosecutor.

The juvenile court administrator manages the staff, budget, and policy for the juvenile court. He or she coordinates the activities of different depart-

Many jobs in the juvenile justice system require long hours of work. This can include researching the case, as well as past cases that were similar to it.

A police officer in Arizona brings a juvenile offender into custody after the juvenile allegedly violated his probation.

ments, such as detention and probation, and acts as a liaison with other agencies and community programs. The juvenile court administrator may serve on boards and task forces that are related to juvenile justice. In some cases, the administrator monitors any research or grant work being conducted in the juvenile court. He or she oversees scheduling, addresses complaints, and resolves conflicts.

In some jurisdictions, juvenile court masters may conduct hearings. Juvenile court masters are lawyers, not judges, and are generally assigned cases that involve lesser offenses or formalities. In busy courts, they can relieve some of the juvenile court judge's workload. Alternate job titles for this type of position include judicial officer, magistrate, referee, hearing officer, and associate judge.

The juvenile court clerk, sometimes called a court case manager or legal administrative assistant, oversees the paperwork involved with the cases being heard in the courtroom. He or she compiles all of the relevant documents prior to the hearing. These might include affidavits, reports, and other files released by different departments and offices. The juvenile court clerk confirms that all of the parties involved in the case are present at the hearing and offers assistance before, during, and after the hearing. Following the hearing, the court clerk distributes copies of the judge's findings and orders. A clerk's specific duties outside of the courtroom vary from one court to another. They may include paralegal work, dealing with the public, and contacting juveniles and their families.

Check the Occupational Outlook Handbook to learn more about the pay for court personnel jobs. The median annual wages for court, municipal, and license clerks, for example, was $39,380 in 2019, and the median annual wages for paralegals and legal assistants was $51,740. Employment in court staff positions was generally projected to increase at a rate equal or above the average rate for all occupations from 2019 to 2029.

CHAPTER 3

JOBS IN PROBATION AND CORRECTIONS

After a juvenile court judge hands down the disposition, the case moves into the oversight of probation and corrections staff. Specialized personnel are trained in managing youth who are put on probation or sentenced to confinement. They'll supervise and participate in the youth's treatment as specified in the terms of the disposition.

A probation officer supervises a juvenile who receives a disposition of probation, the most common disposition in juvenile court. The probation officer can be either an employee of the juvenile justice court or a separate agency. A probation officer's job incorporates both law enforcement and social work as he or she monitors whether the offender is completing the conditions of probation.

A small proportion of offenders receive a disposition of institutional confinement. There's a wide range of different types of juvenile correctional facilities. Staff are sometimes called "correctional officers," but alternate job titles include juvenile caseworker, detention officer, corrections counselor, and juvenile services officer, among others. Job seekers should read the job descriptions closely to see if they match the requirements for the post rather than deciding whether to apply for the position on the job title alone.

A teenager convicted as an adult is escorted by corrections officers. In some states, juveniles convicted as adults can be housed in adult prisons.

LANDMARK LEGISLATION: THE JUVENILE JUSTICE AND DELINQUENCY PREVENTION ACT

There's no single federal juvenile justice system in the United States. Each state administers its own separate system for dealing with juvenile offenders and neglected or dependent children. Young people in similar situations might experience very different outcomes in two different states depending on the laws and treatment methods in each.

In 1974, the Juvenile Justice and Delinquency Prevention Act (JJDPA) was passed by Congress to improve the juvenile justice system. The JJDPA provides federal standards for the care and custody of young offenders, including core requirements for protecting youth in the juvenile justice system. These include measures such as keeping young offenders out of adult facilities and addressing racial and ethnic disparities. The JJDPA funds programs to improve state and local juvenile justice systems, outcomes for offenders, and community safety. The JJDPA also established State Advisory Groups (SAGs) to make recommendations, administer federal funds, and monitor progress on juvenile justice policy. In addition, it created a federal agency called the Office of Juvenile Justice and Delinquency Prevention (OJJDP) that "sponsors research, program, and training initiatives; develops priorities and goals and sets policies to guide federal juvenile justice issues; disseminates information about juvenile justice issues; and awards funds to states to support local programming."

The terms of the JJDPA are not mandatory, but states that don't comply risk losing federal funding. Since being enacted, the JJDPA has been reauthorized and updated seven times.

Young offenders eat breakfast in a community-based youth treatment center in Toledo, Ohio. It serves as an alternative to prison for non-violent youths.

PROBATION OFFICERS

Probation is the most common disposition for juvenile delinquents. Most first-time offenders are put on probation, especially in cases of minor offenses or status offenses. Serious and repeat offenders often receive probation as well. Placement in a juvenile institution, such as large, secure facilities sometimes called schools, is generally reserved for the worst offenders. This is because juvenile institutions have been criticized on the grounds that the institutional environment is more likely to turn lesser offenders into criminals than it is to rehabilitate them. In addition, probation is far less expensive than confinement.

Although the common perception is that a probation officer's job is to oversee offenders who have received their disposition, the officer's role begins much earlier in the process. Probation officers often serve as intake officers. In this capacity, they can recommend diversion when they think it's appropriate.

The probation officer is also responsible for the pre-disposition report. This report describes the juvenile's family life, school history, work history (if any), prior involvement with the juvenile justice system, and any other pertinent information. The probation officer might consult school records, police files, and medical records. He or she may interview the juvenile's family, friends, teachers, police officers, and, when relevant, the victim. After evaluating the facts, the probation officer recommends a disposition to the judge.

During probation, the juvenile must meet specific terms that are intended to promote rehabilitation. The specific terms are left to the discretion of the judge. They generally involve certain requirements (such as completing an anger management course, doing community service, or paying a fine), along with certain restrictions (such as a curfew). Standard probation conditions include staying out of trouble, agreeing to drug testing, keeping in regular contact

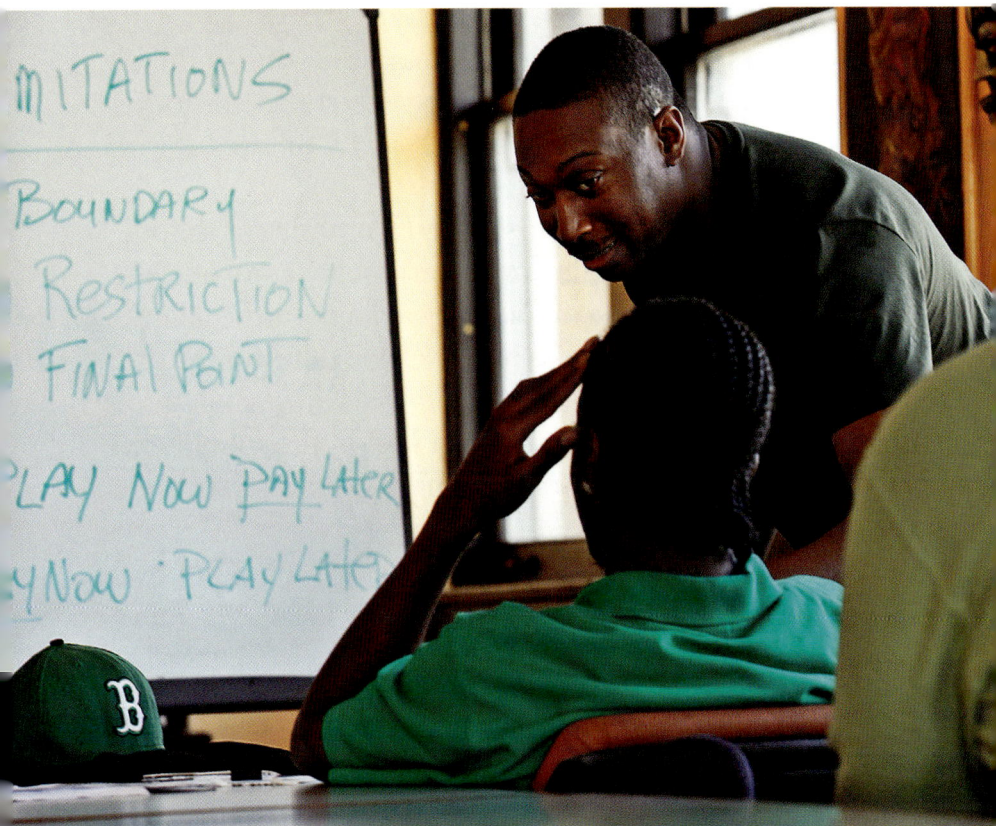

A social services worker talks to teen offenders about plans for getting their lives back on track, emphasizing the importance of work and education.

with the probation officer, and not associating with anyone who has a criminal record.

Probation practices vary from state to state, and probation officers are often on the cutting edge of new approaches to rehabilitation and experimental programs. In some places, serious or repeat offenders might be assigned intensive supervision probation. The probation officer closely monitors the juvenile, both at scheduled meetings and random spot checks. The probation officer also contacts family members, teachers, and other key players in the young offender's life. The offender may be restricted to home, except for approved activities, or he or she may be put under a rigid curfew.

Some states have instituted a practice of school-based probation. The probation officer has an office in a school, where he or she can easily monitor offenders and stay in contact with school administrators. The probation officer also serves as an ambassador of the juvenile justice system within the school and may implement prevention and awareness programs for the general student body.

The probation officer keeps the offender informed of any developments in his or her case and offers counseling and guidance. Probation officers also help offenders obtain services, such as counseling or drug treatment programs, and may provide transportation in some instances. In addition, probation officers supervise aftercare—the juvenile justice equivalent of parole—when a juvenile is released from confinement. Aftercare is intended as a period of supervised readjustment into the community. Many of the conditions for aftercare are similar to probation conditions.

If an offender violates the conditions of probation, then probation can be revoked. When an offender commits a technical violation of probation, the probation officer must deal with the violation as he or she deems appropriate. A technical violation is non-delinquent behavior, such as failing to comply with a treatment plan, skipping a meeting with the

A probation officer, who works closely with school resource officers, talks to one of her students who arrived late to school.

probation officer, or failing to pay restitution. The probation officer will probably let the juvenile off with a warning for a few violations, but repeated violations will probably result in a revocation hearing. If the offender commits another delinquent act, then he or she may be referred for a revocation hearing or sent back to the juvenile court for adjudication. As with the disposition hearing, the probation officer prepares a report that states the facts of the case and recommends a penalty. Options include harsher probation terms or commitment to an institution.

The responsibility for carrying out court orders falls to probation officers. These could involve performing searches, seizing evidence, or making arrests. A probation officer's job can be dangerous, and in some places, probation officers are permitted to carry firearms.

A probation officer must be knowledgeable in juvenile justice laws and procedures, as well as psychology and criminology. He or she must be able to work independently and must have exceptional problem-solving and organization skills. A probation officer might be required to exercise good judgment in stressful situations, such as a family crisis intervention.

Excellent oral and written communication skills are essential to a probation officer's work. The job will present situations that require a range of interpersonal skills: supervising and advising the juvenile; conferring with parents, lawyers, and social services personnel; participating in formal court hearings;

and making presentations to community groups. Although being a probation officer isn't a typical desk job, it does require careful attention to a great deal of paperwork. In addition to the pre-disposition report, the probation officer must manage and update each offender's files and performance reports.

Being a probation officer is a demanding job. Probation officers may find that they carry large caseloads but aren't provided adequate resources to do their work. The job often requires extensive field-work and travel. Probation officers usually choose

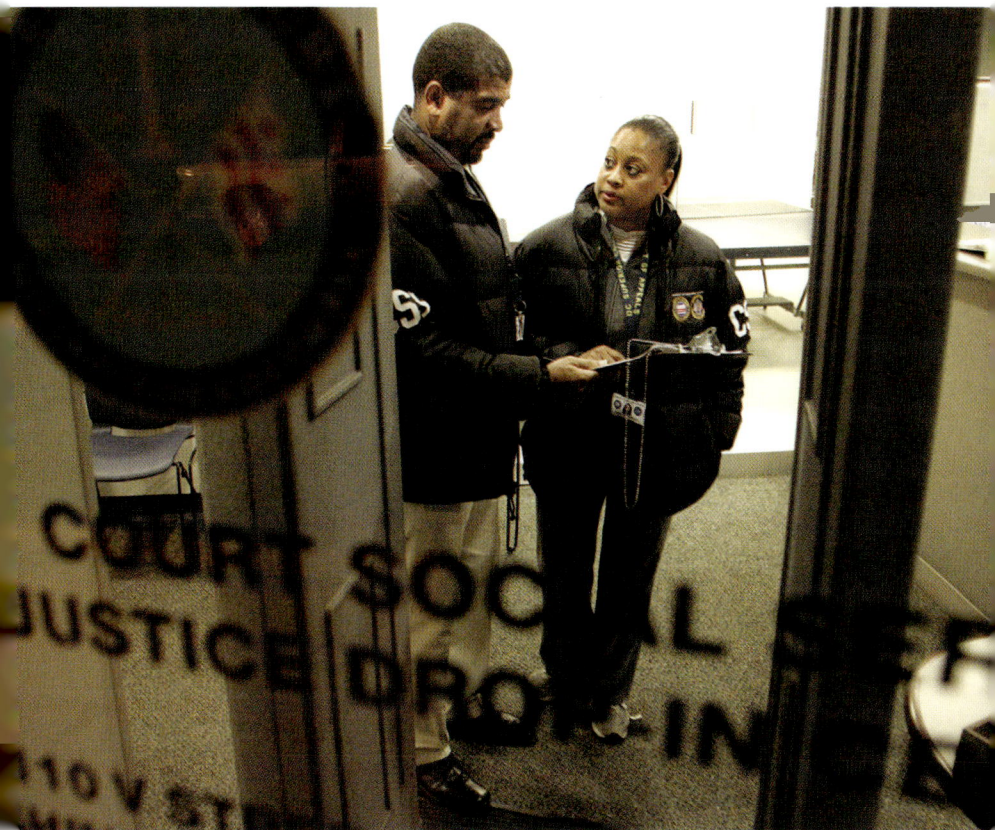

A pair of juvenile parole officers prepare to leave their office in the Social Services department to perform curfew checks on paroled offenders in Washington, D.C.

the field because they want to make a difference in the lives of young people, but they can become frustrated with these kinds of difficulties in carrying out their duties on the job.

Most employers require that probation officers have a four-year degree in criminal justice, in a behavioral science like psychology or sociology, in social work, or in another relevant area. Young people who are just entering the job market can gain relevant experience in activities like volunteer work with at-risk youth or a summer job as a camp counselor. Newly hired probation officers generally receive a period of on-the-job training when they begin work.

About 85 percent of probation officers work directly with offenders. About 15 percent of probation officers are involved in management and administration. These positions require previous job experience and may require higher levels of education or a degree in business or law.

According to the Occupational Outlook Handbook, the median annual wage for probation officers was $54,290 in 2019. Employment in the field was projected to increase 4 percent from 2019 to 2029, which is an average rate for all occupations.

CORRECTIONAL OFFICERS

The number of young offenders in residential placement has dropped steadily since peaking in 2000. According to the Prison Policy Initiative, over

THE MISSOURI APPROACH

Studies have shown that confinement in large correctional facilities fails to rehabilitate juvenile offenders. Many are rearrested and return to the juvenile justice system. Some states have begun to test alternatives to traditional treatment of offenders.

One highly promising model has been successfully implemented in Missouri. The Missouri method works to achieve improvements in behavior that continue after offenders complete the program. Young people receive individualized treatment with a therapeutic approach. Rather than being housed in large institutions far away from their homes, youths are placed in smaller facilities closer to their communities. Families are included in the treatment process. Youths live together in small, closely supervised groups who receive group therapy as well as individual treatment. Staff promote positive interactions between peers, and youths receive guidance in communication skills along with schoolwork. The Missouri approach includes a supervised aftercare program that begins with pre-release planning. Youths are able to make a smooth transition back into school, as well as part-time jobs and extracurricular activities. Some liaise with a community-based mentor as well as their services coordinator.

The Missouri method has proven successful in rehabilitating young offenders. Recidivism rates are significantly lower than in other states. A higher number of offenders achieve academic progress—either toward earning high school credit or completing their GED—than those in traditional juvenile correctional programs. The cost of the Missouri method isn't significantly higher than youth corrections spending in other states. In the long term, the state of Missouri saves significant amounts of money by guiding young offenders away from future involvement in the adult criminal justice system.

108,000 youths were confined in 2000, compared to 43,580 in 2019. Most detained youths were held in detention centers, long-term secure facilities, and residential treatment centers in 2019. Although some facilities are public and others are private, the goal in all cases is to rehabilitate the offender. There are a number of different types of institutions with different goals for the inmates and, as with probation, there's constant experimentation and readjustment in approaches.

The most secure type of institutions are large facilities that include training schools, reformatories, and juvenile correctional facilities. Many are run by the state. These institutions provide education, vocational studies, recreational activities, counseling, and other programs. Nonetheless, the focus on rehabilitation is combined with the goals of deterring delinquency, removing the offenders from the community, and administering appropriate punishment for their actions. Juveniles with serious mental health issues may be sent to a stabilization facility, especially if they're considered to be at a high risk for suicide.

Mid-range offenders may be sent to a juvenile boot-camp program that emphasizes discipline and physical activity. Offenders spend their days following a regimented schedule that's patterned along military lines. While in boot camp, the juveniles also receive education, job training, and counseling. Boot camps are controversial because they haven't been proven to be more effective than traditional pro-

Young offenders who are housed in a youth correctional center walk to the classroom building, escorted by a youth supervisor.

grams. There also have been cases of abuse, overly harsh treatment, and even fatalities at some juvenile camps. Other mid-range offenders may be placed in ranches and wilderness camps. At these "no-locked-doors" facilities in remote areas, young offenders take part in treatment programs and outdoor work, such as conservation projects. Some youths also are housed with other offenders in group homes, a broad community-based treatment placement.

The juvenile justice system sometimes requires that a juvenile be temporarily confined before the adjudication or at other points before beginning the terms of the disposition. These short terms in detention account for the largest numbers of confined juveniles. Juvenile delinquents may be sent to secure detention centers, usually when they're awaiting adjudication or transfer. A delinquent who's received a disposition of commitment to an institution may first be sent to a diagnostic facility. Once there, the juvenile undergoes psychological and medical testing and, in some states, personnel at the diagnostic facility decide which institutional placement is most appropriate. Status offenders, some juvenile delinquents, and neglected or dependent children are more likely to be placed in a youth shelter. Residents at a youth shelter are restricted to the premises, but the facility is unlocked.

By law, juveniles can't be held in adult jails unless there's a "sight and sound separation." In other words, they must be kept safely apart from adult inmates. Juveniles who've been tried and convicted in adult court, however, can be sentenced to adult prison. Depending on state law, these offenders might be held in juvenile facilities until the age of 18 and then transferred to adult prison, held in adult prison but segregated by age, or mixed in with the general prison population. In a practice called blended sentencing, juvenile judges may impose juvenile sanctions to be followed by adult sanctions when the offender turns 18. In this way, judges can require longer periods of confinement for offenders whom they deem deserve harsher punishments.

Juvenile offenders watch television in a common area of the detention facility they are staying in.

The duties of correctional officers vary, depending on the setting, as do the job requirements. But a correctional officer in any institution will benefit from a background working with troubled youth. A correctional officer must be aware that he or she is a role model for the residents, and he or she must have strong communication and supervisory skills. A correctional officer will have to resolve conflicts and manage crises. He or she also has to make safety a priority. In juvenile institutions for serious and violent offenders, extreme precautions are necessary to protect the safety and well-being of the officers and juveniles alike. Everyday tasks include performing inspections, booking new residents into custody, and filling out paperwork. A correctional officer may be required to work night shifts or holidays.

The ideal candidate for a position in juvenile corrections should have a degree in criminal justice, social work, or a related field. But institutions often will hire candidates with a certain amount of relevant college credit or experience. Once hired, the candidate generally starts out as a trainee. He or she receives training in topics such as facility operations, health issues, and juvenile rights. Once the candidate has been promoted to full juvenile correctional officer, he or she may work up the ladder to sergeant and then lieutenant.

Juvenile corrections facilities require administrators, directors, coordinators, supervisors, and other personnel involved in the institution's operation. There may be counselors, recreational therapists, teachers, tutors, and specialists in various treatment programs. Programs such as ranches and forestry camps will also include staff members like youth wilderness instructors. Institutions are held accountable by corrections internal affairs officers and correctional investigators, who ensure policies and rules are followed and juveniles' rights and well-being are protected.

According to the Occupational Outlook Handbook, the median annual wage for correctional officers was $45,180 in 2019. Employment in the field was projected to decrease 7 percent from 2019 to 2029.

CHAPTER 4

RELATED JOBS IN JUVENILE JUSTICE

There are a wide variety of jobs in the field of juvenile justice outside the areas of the court system and corrections. Many different professionals are involved in the complex juvenile justice process beginning with intake and ending with completion of aftercare conditions. This includes law enforcement officers who act as a point of entry into the system and diversion specialists who help youths bypass formal handling in court. In cases that are handled formally, the juvenile may be assigned a court-appointed special advocate (CASA). The youth may work with various treatment specialists, educators, and social workers during the process. They're involved in screening and assessments as well

JANE ADDAMS

Jane Addams (1860–1935) was a pioneer in the field of social work. She was also a progressive reformer and a social philosopher. In 1931, Addams was awarded the Nobel Peace Prize for her activism for international peace.

Addams was born in Cedarville, Illinois, and was one of the first women in the United States to receive a college degree. She's best remembered for founding Hull House in Chicago, a social settlement. Reformers would "settle" in underserved neighborhoods, living and working among the people they aimed to help. Hull House provided educational services, childcare, job training, meeting spaces for groups, a library, and cultural programs. Addams urged practical measures to improve the neighborhood, such as better sanitation, and campaigned for reform on a state and national level. Hull House reformers helped launch the first juvenile court. Addams also advocated for women's rights and helped found the National Association for the Advancement of Colored People (NAACP) and the American Civil Liberties Union (ACLU).

Jane Addams has been called one of America's pioneering social workers for her advocacy of the underprivileged.

as the treatment handed down in a disposition or required as part of a diversion program.

LAW ENFORCEMENT OFFICER

Police officers and other law enforcement officers fight crime and keep the public safe. They enforce laws, preserve the peace, catch criminals, prevent crime, and educate the public about safety and security. They may be called upon to respond to a wide range of situations at a moment's notice. Sometimes, they'll be required to deal with juveniles. These may be juvenile delinquents, status offenders, neglected or dependent children, or victims of crimes.

A police officer should be aware of state and city laws that apply to juveniles, as well as department policies. Juveniles have most of the same constitutional rights as adults, such as the right to remain silent and the right to an attorney when being taken into custody. In addition, many states require that juveniles' parents be contacted when they are detained.

The officer must have probable cause when taking a juvenile into custody. In some cases, this means the officer must be reasonably certain the suspect has committed a crime or was in the process of committing a crime. The officer may establish probable cause through reliable information or through his or her own observation and experience. Officers have a great deal of latitude for taking juveniles into custody, however. An officer may justifiably take a

A law enforcement officer should be familiar with laws and procedures pertaining to juveniles. In some states, for example, a parent or lawyer must be present at police interrogations.

juvenile into custody in circumstances in which it would not be legal to detain an adult. Examples include situations in which the officer believes the youth is in danger or has committed a status offense, such as running away from home.

Police also have a great deal of discretion regarding whether they should formally take the juvenile into custody or deal with him or her more informally instead. They base their decision on factors like the type of offense committed and whether the juvenile has already been involved in the juvenile justice system. If the officer chooses to deal with the situation informally, then he or she is essentially giving the youth a second chance. The simplest option is just to ignore the misbehavior. Another option is to issue a warning and contact the juvenile's parents and/or probation officer. For more serious situations, the officer may take down an official statement and give an official warning. The officer may also refer the juvenile to a social services agency.

Most police officers work as patrol officers who enforce the law on their beat, or assigned area. Some officers, called juvenile officers, specialize in dealing with juveniles and preventing delinquency. In large cities, certain police units may specialize in combating gang activity. Specialized officers receive additional education and training in juvenile justice issues and tactics.

Becoming a police officer is an intensive process that requires rigorous interviews, testing, background checks, and a medical examination. Appli-

A Los Angeles Police Department officer fingerprints a 17-year-old juvenile who was taken into custody and brought to the police station.

cants must have a high school diploma or a GED, and higher levels of education generally give candidates an edge. Once a law enforcement recruit is hired, he or she must attend a police academy. Most recruits start out as patrol officers. After a couple years, they may apply for specialized positions. A job on the police force often requires that officers work nights, weekends, or holidays.

According to the Occupational Outlook Handbook, the median annual wage for police and sheriff's patrol officers was $63,150 in 2019. Employment in the field was projected to increase 5 percent from 2019 to 2029, which is a faster-than-average rate for all occupations.

DIVERSION SPECIALISTS

Minor offenders may be eligible for diversion, which is sometimes called alternative sentencing. These include first-time offenders who've committed non-serious offenses. Examples might include property damage or minor theft, though eligibility for diversion varies from one state to another.

A juvenile diversion specialist—other possible job titles include diversion officer or alternative sentencing specialist—supervises the offender's progress through the diversion program. The process begins with a meeting of the youth, his or her parents, and the diversion specialist. The diversion specialist evaluates the case and sets up an appropriate diversion program. The youth signs a formal

Alyssa Pizarro leads teens in a yoga session inside a pod in a Tacoma, Washington, juvenile detention center as part of the Yoga Behind Bars program.

agreement or contract that states the terms of the program. He or she completes the diversion program under the supervision of a diversion specialist. A diversion program may require community service, restitution (payment for damages or loss), counseling, educational workshops, or writing projects such as an essay or a letter of apology.

The diversion specialist must thoroughly study the juvenile offender's case history before making a recommendation, and the specialist must also monitor the offender's progress as he or she completes the program. The diversion specialist may need to consult with any probation officers, counselors, or court personnel who are involved in the case. The job generally requires that the diversion specialist attend meetings, conduct interviews, act as a liaison, and write reports. A good candidate for a diversion specialist position should have a degree in social work, criminal justice, behavioral science, counseling, or a related field.

ADVOCATING FOR YOUTH

When a youth doesn't have a parent or guardian, the judge may name a court-appointed special advocate (CASA) to represent his or her best interests in court. A CASA is most often involved in cases of dependency or neglect, although CASAs sometimes work on behalf of delinquents. CASAs gather information on the youth, make recommendations in reports, and arrange for the child and family (if there is one) to receive social services. Many are volunteers, though requirements for a CASA differ from one state to another. Often, CASA programs are run by court staff members, which can include lawyers and social workers, as well as volunteers.

Courts also may appoint an advocate for the victim of juvenile crime. The victim advocate explains the procedures of the juvenile court and keeps the victim informed of developments in the case. If the offender goes to court, the advocate accompanies the victim to court hearings. The advocate helps that person file a victim impact statement, which may include a request for restitution. Usually, the victim advocate works for the prosecutor's office or for the probation department.

One approach intended to help both the offender and the victim is a model called restorative justice, which is a form of conflict resolution. The parties involved or affected by the offense come to an agreement on how the offender can work to undo the harm that he or she has caused. Restorative justice programs often are recommended as diversion and aren't formal court proceedings. Participation is voluntary for the victim. The victim shouldn't be pressured to take part.

Restorative justice often takes the form of mediation between the offender, his or her parents or guardians, and the victim. A trained mediator assists them. The victim has a chance to describe the impact of the offense and try to understand the juvenile's motivations. The offender must directly face the real

PROVIDING SOCIAL SERVICES

Social workers help people handle the difficulties and challenges that arise in their lives. Their clients' issues might involve mental or physical health problems, substance abuse, domestic violence, financial troubles, or relationship problems. Social workers assess the client's situation and needs. They research available resources, advocate for services on the client's behalf, and refer the client to other agencies and programs. Social workers also may intervene in crisis situations. Some social workers, called clinical social workers, diagnose and treat mental and behavioral disorders.

A child in the juvenile justice system may work with a child and family social worker. He or she works with families to help ensure that children will have a stable and healthy home environment. The social worker may refer a family to childcare resources, food assistance, substance abuse treatment, or counseling. He or she may intervene in cases of abuse or neglect. Some social workers also work in schools with at-risk children.

An aspiring social worker should have great communication, organization, and problem-solving skills. Most positions require at least a bachelor's degree in social work or a related major. Many states also require social workers to be licensed. Social workers are qualified to work in a variety of positions providing services to people in need. Other possible job titles include caseworker, child advocate, service coordinator, or family and youth specialist.

According to the Occupational Outlook Handbook, the median annual wages for child, family, and school social workers was $47,390 in 2019. The job outlook for social workers was positive—overall employment of social workers was projected to grow 13 percent from 2019 to 2029, much faster than the average for all occupations.

consequences of the offense. All parties come to an agreement on appropriate penalty, such as restitution or community service. This process is intended to allow all parties to benefit from involvement with the juvenile justice system.

An option available for some youths dealing with drug offenses is juvenile drug court. Drug courts are often viewed as a diversion program rather than a formal adjudication. Drug courts were developed as a way to intervene more efficiently and effectively in cases of teen drug use. Regular juvenile court

Teens share their thoughts and feelings during a group therapy session. Programs such as therapy and counseling help offenders reach the end goal of successful rehabilitation.

often fails to place drug users in treatment programs quickly enough. Drug courts require the participation of family members, drug or alcohol counselors, and sometimes representatives from school and community organizations. The process often is more intensive than that of traditional juvenile court, and the judge holds frequent hearings to monitor the juvenile's progress.

TREATMENT AND EDUCATION OPTIONS

Whether an offender is dealt with formally or informally, the end goal of the juvenile justice system is generally rehabilitation. Many juvenile delinquents are required to attend counseling as part of their treatment program. Counselors may work directly for the juvenile justice system through a court or another institution. They also may work for other branches of the social welfare system or for private organizations. Typically, counselors are required to have a degree in counseling, behavioral sciences, or social work. Psychologists may be required to hold a graduate degree in psychology or counseling.

A delinquent's treatment program is tailored to his or her needs. It may include individual and group therapy, education, prevention programs, or crisis intervention. Family counseling sessions address issues in the youth's home life that contributed to his or her delinquency. Substance abuse counselors help juveniles with alcohol, tobacco, or drug problems. Youths may be required to take anger management

Teens share their thoughts and feelings during a group therapy session. Programs such as therapy and counseling help offenders reach the end goal of successful rehabilitation.

classes. Sex offenders are generally required to complete an intensive program that addresses their attitudes and behavior patterns. Youths with mental health issues meet with mental health specialists or psychologists to deal with their issues. Delinquents who are confined to an institution may participate in programs designed by a recreational therapist.

A juvenile's disposition may require that he or she participate in day or evening treatment programs. These programs may be appropriate for juveniles who need strict supervision. They also can serve as an aftercare measure for juveniles who've been released from confinement. Juveniles who aren't enrolled in school attend day treatment programs. They may receive counseling, life skills training, and educational support. Youths who are enrolled in school attend similar evening treatment programs. These programs require skilled, caring, and dedicated counselors who are strict but fair and compassionate. Above all, they must be committed to the well-being and reform of juvenile offenders.

In addition, delinquent youths often pursue educational and job training opportunities while they work their way through the juvenile justice system. Teachers employed by juvenile justice programs should have a degree in education and, in some cases, state certification. Delinquents who aren't enrolled in school may participate in literacy classes, tutoring, vocational training, remedial education, GED preparatory classes, or other types of classes depending on their needs. Employment counselors

Emanuel Martinez and assistant Arturo Ballesteros look over a mural being painted at a youth services center in Golden, Colorado, where incarcerated youth volunteers are helping to complete six murals.

may offer guidance in finding a job and making the transition to working life.

JUVENILE NEGLECT AND DEPENDENCY CASES

Most examinations of the juvenile justice system focus on the treatment of delinquents. Neglected and dependent youth, however, aren't involved with the system due to delinquent criminal acts. Instead, they fall under the jurisdiction of the juvenile court because of the conduct of their parents or guardians. Examples of neglect include physical, emotional, and educational neglect, as well as physical, sexual, and emotional abuse. Dependent youths are those who must rely on the court because their parents are incapable of caring for them, usually because of physical or mental disability.

When there's a report of child neglect or abuse, the case is investigated by the child welfare system. Nationally, the agency responsible for child welfare is the Children's Bureau, which is part of the U.S. Department of Health and Human Services. There also are state and local agencies, such as child protective services or social services departments, which are responsible for child welfare. Government agencies work together with private and community organizations.

If the case meets the legal definition of dependency or neglect, then child protective services workers investigate and assess the situation. The youth isn't removed from the home unless a caseworker believes he or she is in immediate danger. In most cases, dependency and neglect cases are dealt with informally. The child welfare system helps families resolve the causes of the situation. In most cases, the ultimate goal is to keep families together or, if the child has been removed from the home, to reunite families.

If the informal options fail, or if there are special considerations, then a case of dependency or neglect goes before juvenile court. (Criminal charges for the guardians, such as severe abuse, are dealt with sep-

A caseworker's main goal is to help the child and keep them safe. In most cases, the aim is to keep families together.

arately in adult court.) The judge rules whether the evidence supports the allegations of dependency or neglect. If the allegations are found to be true, the judge hands down a disposition. The youth may be returned to his or her family. He or she may be placed in foster care, either with a relative or with a family that's been appointed by the child protective services agency. The youth's parents could lose custody.

Child protective services workers—other possible job titles include child protective services specialists, child welfare workers, or child protective investigators—have the responsibility of investigating and reviewing reports of abuse and neglect. They must have a thorough understanding of state laws and procedures concerning child protection. They must also be able to recognize symptoms of abuse.

Youths who are placed in the custody of child protective services are assigned a caseworker. If the youth is placed in foster care, the caseworker makes sure the home is suitable. He or she may find a new placement for the youth if it becomes necessary. When the goal is reunification with the family, the caseworker arranges family visits and monitors the family's progress in fulfilling the conditions for reunification. When the goal is adoption, the caseworker helps the adoptive family with arrangements. He or she reports progress toward the youth's goal to the court. The caseworker also offers counseling to families and to the youth, and he or she acts as a liaison between the different agencies and organizations.

Jobs such as juvenile diversion specialists, substance abuse and mental health treatment specialists, and child protective services workers are described in the Occupational Outlook Handbook in categories such as probation officers, therapists, and social workers. Check out the handbook for information on pay as well as more details about the requirements and responsibilities of each job.

CHAPTER 5

GETTING READY FOR A JUVENILE JUSTICE CAREER

Candidates interested in working in the juvenile justice system have a wide variety of specialization to consider. Professionals such as lawyers, psychologists, and policy makers must hold advanced degrees. Many of the specialists who provide services such as mental health or substance abuse treatment must complete appropriate training and certification. But there are also opportunities for candidates with a high school degree along with some training and related experience. People who want to make a crucial difference in the lives of young people should manage to find a niche that matches their aptitudes and interests.

Caroline Raymond poses for a photo at the Long Creek Youth Development Center in South Portland, Maine, two months after taking over as superintendent of the juvenile detention facility.

Just as there are many different types of careers in juvenile justice, there is great variety in hours and types of workplaces. Court personnel and legal professionals typically work nine-to-five jobs in the courthouse. Probation officers often travel extensively and sometimes work late-afternoon and evening hours. Sometimes, they remain on call in case one of their probationers gets into trouble. Correctional officers work at various kinds of institutions, and they may work night shifts, weekends, and/or holidays.

YOUTH SUPPORT AND OUTREACH PROGRAMS

As seen, there are a great variety of career paths within the juvenile justice system, many of which are government jobs. But there also are great opportunities with non-profit organizations and other non-government programs that provide services for at-risk youth. The juvenile justice system may refer some offenders to youth outreach programs for treatment and support—most centers must be licensed and accredited for the services they provide.

A youth outreach organization may offer services such as mental health treatment, substance abuse treatment, diversion programs, health services, employment assistance, and foster care placement. Some programs reach out to specific at-risk groups, such as racial minorities, LGBTQ+ youth, or homeless youth. Many youth outreach programs provide services to young people in their late teens or early twenties who may no long qualify for government services provided to minors, as well. Youth outreach programs may employ therapists, treatment specialists, social workers, health care professionals, and case managers, as well as a variety of support positions. Many organizations also have internship and volunteer opportunities.

THE SUCCESSFUL JOB SEARCH

In every area of juvenile justice, a candidate must have relevant education, training, and experience for the job. College majors such as criminal justice, behavioral sciences, counseling, or social work provide a solid foundation for many juvenile justice jobs.

There also are many different ways that job seekers interested in juvenile justice can gain relevant experience. Many juvenile justice programs accept volunteers to work with young offenders or assist with administrative tasks. Other opportunities exist at community groups, schools, hospitals, libraries, churches, police departments, athletic associations, and many other organizations that involve children and young adults. Volunteers may tutor students, act as mentors, plan activities, chaperone field trips, help lead workshops, or work with children in other ways. Students may take a summer job working with kids, such as a camp counselor, or complete internships related to juvenile justice.

Once a job seeker has chosen a field within juvenile justice, the next step is the job search. When searching online, a job seeker should look at general job listing websites as well as the specific sites of potential employers. Most juvenile justice agencies have a "Career Opportunities" section on their website. Some sites for professional associations—such as correctional associations—also list job openings. Recent college graduates may find job leads through their school's career center.

Finally, a serious job seeker should visit possible employers and set up informational interviews. Even if they're not hiring at the time, these employers may be able to give tips about other prospective job openings in the area and offer you up-close insights into the work being done there. Informational interviews are an invaluable way to make contacts in your field of choice. The person you speak to may know someone who's hiring or may remember you six months later when he or she is trying to fill a newly vacant position.

Most employers require that job seekers send a résumé and cover letter when applying for a position. Government departments also may require an application form. A résumé serves as an introduction to prospective employers. An effective résumé provides relevant information that demonstrates the candidate is a good fit for the job opening. On their résumé, job seekers should describe skills and experience gained from past employment, education, or activities, rather than just listing job titles. It's often a good idea for job seekers to tailor their résumé to each employer. The cover letter gives job seekers a chance to elaborate on the reasons why they're a great fit for the job.

Employers generally pay close attention to an applicant's employment history, but young people and recent graduates just starting out in the workplace don't have an extensive work history. When this is the case, applicants should emphasize related education and experiences that make them stand

A job interview is a candidate's chance to persuade the interviewer that she's the best fit for the job. In addition, it's an opportunity to learn more about the workplace.

out from the rest of the candidates. Job seekers should open a résumé with their strengths, whether it's an impressive employment record or extensive volunteer work.

The next step is the job interview. There are many books and online resources available that give interview tips. Before the interview, the candidate should research the employer and prepare a list of questions about the organization and the

"SEARCH AND SEIZURE" IN SCHOOLS

Sometimes, landmark cases can affect the everyday lives of ordinary people, even teens in high school. In 1985, the Supreme Court issued a ruling on the case of *New Jersey v. T.L.O.*, in which a school administrator searched the purse of a 14-year-old student on the suspicion that she had been smoking. He found cigarettes, marijuana, and rolling papers.

The girl's lawyers argued the evidence was inadmissible in court because the administrator's actions violated the teen's Fourth Amendment rights against "unreasonable search and seizure." The Supreme Court decided against her, ruling that the administrator had reasonable suspicion to perform a search. The court also stated that students weren't entitled to full constitutional protections in school as they were in other settings, in order to maintain a safe learning environment.

As a result of *New Jersey v. T.L.O.* and other court rulings, searches in school are generally legal if there are reasonable grounds, although laws and policies vary from one state or school to another. School searches continue to evolve with the times. Today, students participating in athletics may be required to take random drug tests. Issues such as cell phone searches and access to social media accounts have been taken up in courts cases.

job. The candidate should use his or her research to demonstrate solid knowledge of the company, court, or institution during the interview. Employees who work with children often are required to undergo a background check and sometimes a drug test. Most job seekers don't land a job on their very first interview, but every interview is a learning experience that better prepares you for the next interview. With persistence, a qualified and enthusiastic candidate is sure to find a good match in the field.

Depending on state law, school officials may have the legal right to search possessions belonging to students.

CURRENT AND FUTURE ISSUES IN JUVENILE JUSTICE

As long as there are youths in need of rehabilitation and state services, there'll be jobs for professionals in the field of juvenile justice. Nevertheless, the juvenile justice system is in a state of constant transformation and reform. Policy makers recognize new needs and update the programs that serve delinquent and neglected youth. Ongoing research is performed to help understand the root causes of juvenile delinquency and the effectiveness of various approaches to treatment and rehabilitation. New insights will inform future innovations in juvenile justice.

The juvenile justice system also will continue to grapple with the consequences of factors outside its control. Child poverty is a huge issue for many youths in the juvenile justice system. During economic downturns, the budget for child welfare spending often is subject to cuts in funding. The COVID-19 pandemic that began in 2020 destabilized the lives of children across the country. Many children experienced economic hardship, the pandemic disrupted the foster care system, and outbreaks of COVID-19 occurred in some juvenile facilities.

Landmark court cases and updated legislation from the 2010s will continue to shape new policies and programs. In the 2010 case of *Graham v. Florida*, the Supreme Court found that sentencing juvenile offenders to life in prison without parole for cases other than murder is unconstitutional.

The court stated that such sentences were cruel and unusual, and that they deprived the offender of the "chance to demonstrate growth and maturity."

Two years later, in the 2012 case of *Miller v. Alabama*, the Supreme Court made another landmark ruling on juvenile sentencing. In 2006, Evan Miller was found guilty of a murder he committed at the age of 14. The sentence was a mandatory life in prison without parole. The Supreme Court reversed lower court decisions that found the sentence constitutional. As in previous cases, the court noted that it constituted cruel and unusual punishment, being as psychology had shown that juveniles are fundamentally different from adults. The 2016 Supreme Court ruling in the *Montgomery v. Louisiana* case applied the *Miller* decision retroactively. Therefore, offenders sentenced to life in prison without parole before 2016 for crimes committed as juveniles are entitled to resentencing.

In 2018, Congress passed the Juvenile Justice Reform Act, reauthorizing and revising the Juvenile Justice and Delinquency Prevention Act that was originally created in 1974. It was the first time legislators had revisited the JJDPA since 2002. Reformers praised the strengthened protections for young offenders in the reauthorization. The terms required states to comply with certain requirements in order to receive federal funding.

The legislation reaffirmed and amended four core provisions intended to protect youths in the juvenile justice system. The first restricts the circumstances in which status offenders can be locked up in detention or confinement. Juveniles who commit offenses such as truancy, running away, violating curfew, or use of alcohol should be treated through community-based services rather than confinement.

The second provision requires that most youth be removed from adult jails and prisons, with limited exceptions. Young people housed alongside adults have been found to suffer psychological and physical consequences. They're more likely to attempt suicide or be assaulted by staff or other inmates. This doesn't include juveniles being tried as adults for felony offenses.

The third provision addresses the circumstances in which juveniles may be held in adult jails or prisons, such as limited time periods before or after a court hearing or slightly longer times in rural areas. The facility must maintain sight and sound separation between juveniles and adults.

The fourth requires that states identify and address racial and ethnic disparities in their juvenile justice systems. Youths of color are overrepresented in the juvenile justice system compared to the general population. Some studies have shown that youths of color are more likely to receive harsher sentences.

The Juvenile Justice Reform Act included certain other requirements that protect young offenders and promote rehabilitation. For example, certain types of restraints, particularly for pregnant youths, as well as dangerous practices, such as unreasonable isolation, were eliminated. States must draw up re-entry

Juvenile offenders wait outside the gym at a Toledo, Ohio, juvenile detention center. When possible, the county promotes community-based treatment allowing youths to live at home and attend school.

plans for confined offenders being released. It calls for increasing screening and treatment for mental health and substance abuse issues.

Individual states also have been working to reform their juvenile justice systems. Generally, they're trending toward diversion rather than prosecution, and community-based treatment rather than confinement. Many states have ended or reduced confinement for status offenses as well as minor or nonviolent offenses. In 2019, California announced the closure of its Department of Juvenile

From judges and lawyers to counselors and social workers, there are many careers to choose from in the juvenile justice system.

Justice facilities. Evidence-based programs have shown that alternatives to confinement can lead to better outcomes.

Although it might sound like the juvenile justice system is in a state of flux, there will always be career opportunities for dedicated professionals in the field who want to work to give young people a second chance. People who work in the field of juvenile justice have the satisfaction of seeing at-risk youth begin to thrive due to their efforts. There are many benefits experienced by those with a career in juvenile justice, including the knowledge that they make a difference in the lives of young people in the course of their everyday work.

GLOSSARY

adjudication: The process in which a judge rules whether the allegations of delinquent conduct are true or denied (guilty or not guilty).

allegation: An accusation; specifically, a court accusation against a juvenile offender.

appeal: To apply for review of a case or particular issue to a higher court.

arson: The crime of intentionally setting fire to a building or other property.

bench: The seat for the judge in a courtroom; also, a symbol for the office and authority of a judge.

community service: Work performed by offenders as part of their sentence.

custody: Legal restraint or detention; also, guardianship, such as in a child custody case.

delinquency: The violation of a law by a juvenile.

discretion: The power of a judge or other official to make judgments based on principles of law and fairness.

disposition: The final determination in a case; the juvenile justice equivalent of a sentence.

diversion: A type of informal probation in which the case is not formally processed by the juvenile court.

evidence: Data presented in court as proof of facts in a case.

expungement: The act of erasing or canceling out.

jurisdiction: The right or power to administer justice.

probation: The act of suspending an offender's sentence and allowing him or her to go free subject to certain conditions.

rebuttal: The presentation of opposing evidence or arguments.

rehabilitation: The restoration of an offender to a law-abiding individual.

restitution: Money or services given in compensation of loss or injury.

status offense: Conduct that is illegal for a juvenile but non-criminal for an adult.

testify: To state or declare under oath, usually in a court of law.

waiver: The act of relinquishing a right, claim, or privilege.

FOR MORE INFORMATION

Council of Juvenile Justice Administrators (CJJA)

350 Granite St. Suite 1203
Braintree, MA 02184
(781) 843-2663
Website: cjja.net/
Twitter: @cjca_pbs

The Council of Juvenile Justice Administrators is a nonprofit organization that works to improve juvenile correctional services, programs, and practices.

Juvenile Law Center (JLC)

1800 JFK Blvd, Suite #1900B
Philadelphia, PA 19103
(215) 625-0551
Website: www.jlc.org
Facebook: @JuvenileLawCenter
Instagram, Twitter: @juvlaw1975

The Juvenile Law Center is a nonprofit legal service that advocates children's rights in court, supports policy reform, and provides education and training resources.

National Center for Juvenile Justice (NCJJ)

3700 South Water Street, Suite 200
Pittsburgh, PA 15203
(412) 227-6950
Website: www.ncjj.org

The research division of the National Council of Juvenile and Family Court Judges, the National Center for Juvenile Justice conducts studies and provides information related to juvenile justice.

National Juvenile Defender Center (NJDC)
1350 Connecticut Avenue NW Suite 304
Washington, D.C., 20036
(202) 452-0010
Website: njdc.info/
Facebook: @NJCD.info
Instagram: @natjuvdefend
Twitter: @NatJuvDefend
The National Juvenile Defender Center provides information
and resources for defense attorneys representing children in
the juvenile justice system.

Office of Juvenile Justice and Delinquency Prevention (OJJDP)
810 7th Street NW
Washington, D.C., 20531
(202) 307-5911
Website: ojjdp.ojp.gov/
Facebook, Twitter: @OJPOJJDP
A branch of the U.S. Department of Justice, the Office of Juvenile Justice and Delinquency Prevention supports states and
local governments and provides services to fulfill its mission
of promoting juvenile delinquency prevention and improving
the juvenile justice system.

Youth Justice
Government of Canada
Website: www.canada.ca/en/services/policing/
justice/youth.html
Canada's government website explains the country's youth
justice system and provides updates on government action
related to juvenile justice.

FOR FURTHER READING

Barrington, Richard. *The Juvenile Court System: Your Legal Rights*. New York, NY: Rosen Publishing, 2016.

Bolles, Richard N. *What Color Is Your Parachute? 2021: Your Guide to a Lifetime of Meaningful Work and Career Success (Revised)*. Berkeley, CA: Ten Speed Press, 2020.

Johnston, Coy H. *Careers in Criminal Justice, 2nd ed.* Thousand Oaks, CA: SAGE Publications, Inc., 2019.

Johnston, Coy H. *Careers in Law Enforcement*. Thousand Oaks, CA: SAGE Publications, Inc., 2017.

Klutz, Douglas. *Career Guide in Criminal Justice*. New York, NY: Oxford University Press, 2018.

Meyer, Terry Teague. *Juvenile Detention Centers: Your Legal Rights*. New York, NY: Rosen Publishing, 2016.

Mijares, Tomas C. *Careers for the Criminal Justice Major: A Practical Guide to Course Selection, Description of Entry-Level Positions and Best Prospects for Career Development*. Springfield, IL: Charles C Thomas Publisher, Ltd., 2018.

Nagle, Cristen. *Your Legal Rights as a Juvenile Tried as an Adult.* New York, NY: Rosen Publishing, 2015.

Pryor, Jeffrey W. *Compassionate Careers: Making a Living by Making a Difference.* Pompton Plains, NJ: Career Press, 2015.

Ritter, Jessica A. *101 Careers in Social Work.* New York, NY: Springer Publishing Company, 2015.

INDEX

A

Addams, Jane, 61

adjudication, 8, 9, 11, 14, 15, 17, 24, 28, 30, 31, 32, 34, 38, 50, 56

adult court, 4, 6, 8, 9, 10, 11, 15, 17, 18, 28, 33, 34, 53, 77, 78

aftercare, 16, 17, 48, 53, 60, 74

alcohol, 12, 20, 72, 90

American Civil Liberties Union (ACLU), 61

anger management, 46, 72

B

boot camp, 15, 54, 56

C

caseworker, 22, 76, 77

Children's Bureau, 76

child welfare worker, 5, 78, 79

college degree, 26, 27, 34, 52, 58, 61, 66, 68, 70, 72, 74, 80, 83

community service, 14, 15, 46, 68, 71

Congress, 44, 89

Constitution, 20, 21

correctional officer, 5, 22, 42, 43, 52, 54, 58, 59, 82

counseling, 5, 15, 23, 48, 53, 54, 58, 68, 72, 74, 82, 83

court-appointed special advocate (CASA), 60, 68, 69

court staff (personnel), 5, 24, 25, 34, 37, 38, 68, 69, 82

COVID-19, 88

curfew, 12, 13, 46, 48, 90

D

day treatment program, 15, 74

death penalty, 20

defense attorney, 28, 30, 31, 32, 33, 34

Department of Health and Human Services, 76

ABOUT THE AUTHOR

Corona Brezina is an author who has written over a dozen young adult books for Rosen Publishing. Several of her previous books have also focused on legal and social issues concerning teens, including *Personal Freedom and Civic Duty: Understanding Equal Rights and Financing* and *Conducting a Political Campaign*. She lives in Chicago.

CREDITS